June
Moon

by Kathleen Souza
Illustrated by Hannah Robidoux

ISBN: 978-1-61296-871-1
PUBLISHED BY BLACK ROSE WRITING
www.blackrosewriting.com

Printed in the United States of America
June Moon is printed in Myriad Pro

For my cherished "hatchlings" - Katie and Danny

FOREWORD

Moonlight aids female sea turtles who come ashore to nest, and it helps to orient hatchlings when they travel from those nests back to the sea.

Female sea turtles will crawl from the sea, usually at night, to a dry part of the beach. Not only will they often appear on the same beach, they often return within a few hundred yards of where they last nested. They will begin to fling away loose sand with their flippers to create a hole, or chamber, for the eggs. When a turtle has finished digging the egg chamber, she begins to lay her eggs. The group of eggs is called a clutch. Once all the eggs are in the chamber, or nest, the mother turtle uses her rear flippers to push sand into it. Gradually, she packs the sand down over the top to disguise the nest. By throwing sand in all directions, it is much harder for predators to find the eggs. After the nest is thoroughly concealed, the female crawls back to the sea. It is important that sea turtles are never disturbed during this nesting process.

The baby turtles, called hatchlings, emerge from the nest as a group. Digging out of the nest can take several days. Hatchlings usually emerge from their nest at night. The little turtles orient themselves to the brightest horizon and then dash toward the sea.

FOREWORD

If they don't make it to the ocean quickly, many hatchlings will die of dehydration in the sun or be caught by predators like birds and crabs. Once in the water, they typically swim several miles off shore, where they are caught in currents and seaweed that may carry them for years before returning to nearshore waters.

The threats facing sea turtles are numerous. Humans and other animals pose a threat to sea turtles and hatchlings. In many states where sea turtles nest, state laws and regulations have been passed to protect them and their habitat. Field work is at the heart of sea turtle conservation, and, fortunately, there are many protected sights where data is collected, local conservation strategies are devised, and humans monitor and help to protect the nesting process and the hatchlings. This story takes place in one of these important, protected areas.

Twinkles of light shone on the white-capped waves as she rolled out of the sea. She began to trudge across the beach as the clouds parted, and the moon lit a path for the mother turtle. She made her way to the spot she had been before, the place to which she now returned. She was searching for that perfect stretch of sand for her new nest.

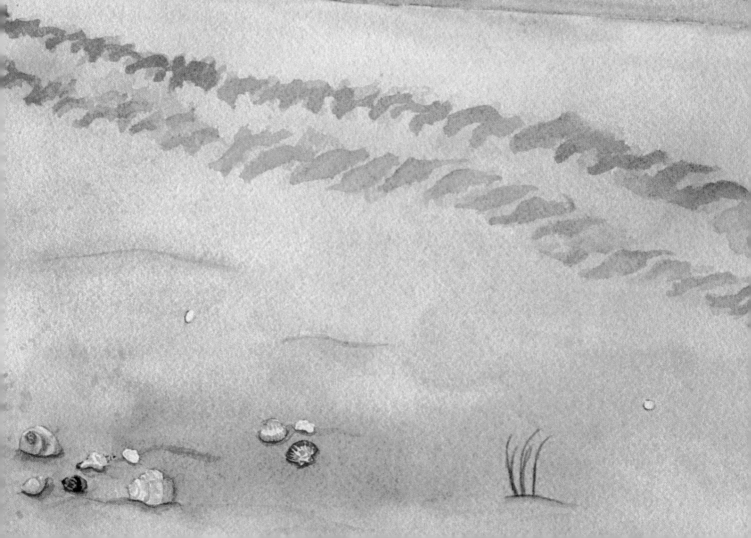

It took most of the night as mother turtle found her spot, laid her clutch of eggs, and hid them under the sand. Then, exhausted, she returned to the sea.

It is several weeks later, and the June moon is rising over the sea. In the warm nest under the sand, a baby turtle and the rest of the clutch seem to waken. He feels snug and secure inside his shell, but the feeling that it is time to move and rise is getting stronger and stronger. As he stirs, there are sudden pops and cracks.

The warm sand shifts and tiny grains sift by him as he releases from his egg and crawls upward and out - on to the sand and into the air and light of the June moon. The air is damp; it is almost as wet as the sea. The top sand is cool, but Little Turtle is burning with the desire to travel to the glistening horizon of water, topped by the moon, which is softly rippling at the edge of the sand in the distance.

"The water is so far away," he thinks. "There's nothing but sand and air up here. There's nothing to hold on to." He hesitates. "How will I make the long journey and stay safe?"

As he looks around, he sees other hatchlings appearing from the nest. "We were safe in that small place, and now I may never feel that security again." He is saddened by this thought, but his sadness turns to relief when the other hatchlings gather around him as the June moon casts shadows on their small prints in the cool sand.

"How are we to make it to our ocean home?" they ask. "We hear the sea, but how can we travel that far and remain safe?" They all look towards the bright moon and the shimmering waves in the distance.

Little Turtle nods. He also knows that dangers surround them. "We have to make a plan for where we are right now and what we have, which is each other. Stay close together. We can travel this distance, but we must depend on one another. We must protect and trust each other."

At first he had been afraid. When you're alone, everything feels uncertain. Now, with the hatchlings beside him, he feels courageous and determined. Friendship is real and true when it makes you feel safe, and now Little Turtle feels certain that as long as he and the hatchlings stay together, they can be safe.

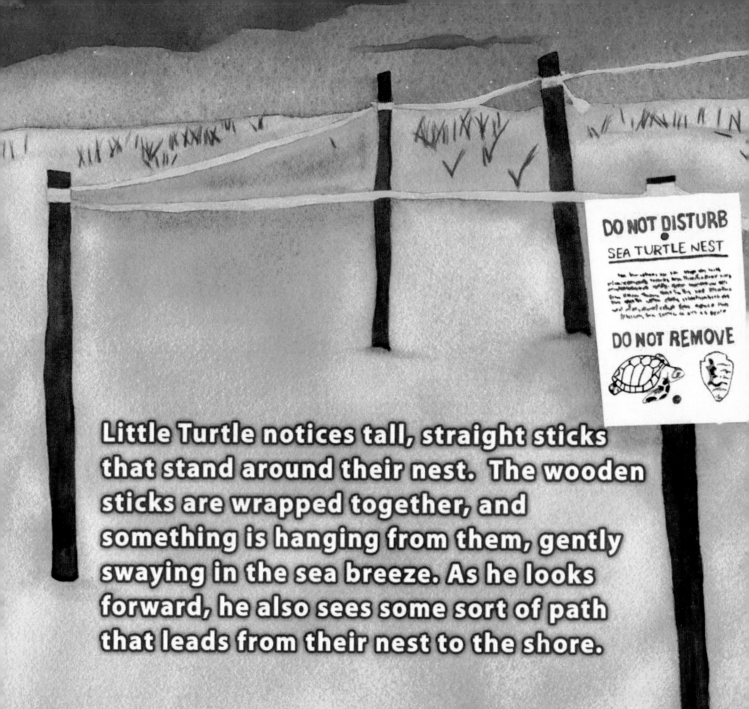

DO NOT DISTURB

SEA TURTLE NEST

DO NOT REMOVE

Little Turtle notices tall, straight sticks that stand around their nest. The wooden sticks are wrapped together, and something is hanging from them, gently swaying in the sea breeze. As he looks forward, he also sees some sort of path that leads from their nest to the shore.

He is puzzled. It looks like a path made just for the hatchlings. His heart quickens at this new sight. It seems that along with each other, they have more help. This extra help is unexpected, and Little Turtle is excited and grateful.

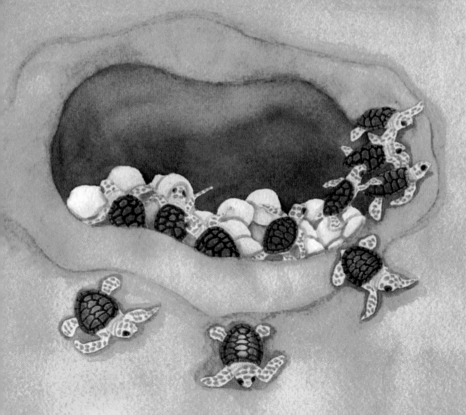

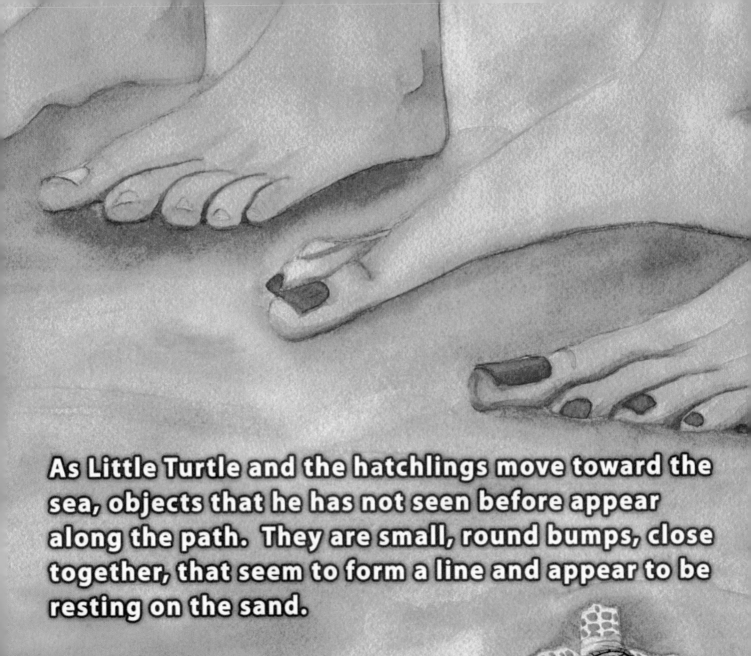

As Little Turtle and the hatchlings move toward the sea, objects that he has not seen before appear along the path. They are small, round bumps, close together, that seem to form a line and appear to be resting on the sand.

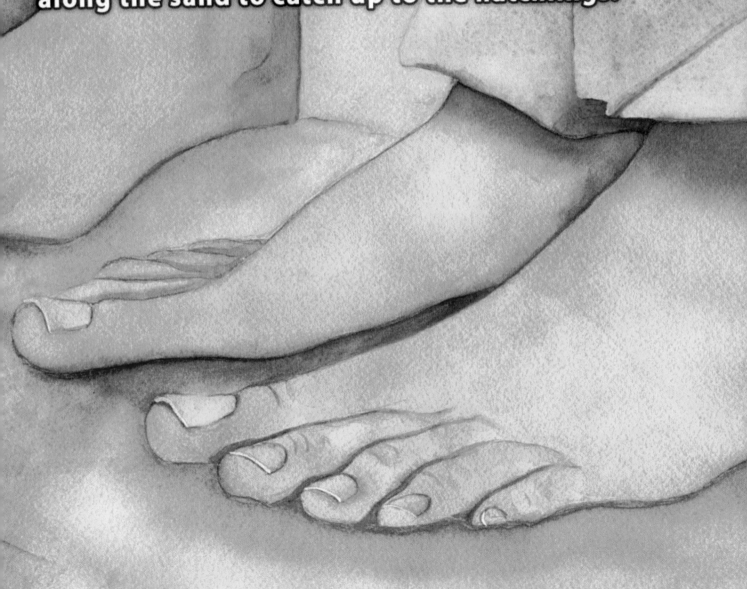

The hatchlings begin to scurry to the sea, but Little Turtle pauses to examine the objects. "We will help you move forward," he hears a voice whisper. The unexpected voice startles him, and he scurries along the sand to catch up to the hatchlings.

"What was that? Friend or danger?" he wonders. As he considers the answer to this question, the air above begins to fill with loud, screeching sounds, and there is a whirl of movement. Looking up he sees a flurry of white feathers glowing in the moonlight, their dark shadows circling below.

There is chaos in the movement - sideways – up and down - all around - and it gets closer. Suddenly there is panic as large birds, with their mouths wide open, dive toward Little Turtle and the group of hatchlings.

But, just as quickly, there are loud noises and whistles. Little Turtle watches as some of the bumps leave the edge of the path. The noise grows louder, and there is movement and thumping in the sand.

"Seagulls!" he hears. "Don't let them near! Run! Wave your arms! Make lots of noise! We must protect the turtles!" And just as quickly as it had appeared, the screeching and fluttering chaos moves down the sandy shore and into the moonlit night.

Although he is still not sure what happened, he knows how frightened it made him feel, and Little Turtle is sure that they have just escaped a real danger. The "bumps" helped keep them safe and moving forward, and he knows now that these are friends. "They have helped build a safe path to my future," he realizes.

Knowing that these new friends are staying right beside him, encouraging and protecting him, gives Little Turtle the assurance he needs. He sees that many of the hatchlings, also frightened by the commotion, are moving faster, and he and his group are nearing the water's edge. Little Turtle also sees that the bumps have returned to the barrier, and with a sense of confidence and determination, he, too, scurries to the nearby shore that is glowing in the moonlight.

The sparkling water pulls forward and back, waving him on and welcoming him in. Little Turtle watches as the hatchlings in front of him, one-by-one, disappear into the cool, inviting water.

The crests of the waves shimmer in the light of the June moon, and the small turtle shells twinkle among them. They stayed together, and they have made it safely. He feels the tug of a wave, but he hesitates.

He takes one last look at the friends behind him and then moves forward with the friends before him. The moonlit waves of that far-away shore are now right in front of him.

Little Turtle thinks how lucky they are to have arrived safely. He knows it was because of the togetherness of the hatchlings and the unexpected help of his new friends. Staying together kept them safe and moving forward, and now his new world is ready and waiting.

Little Turtle spreads his small flippers and eases into a gently rippling wave, already imagining himself eating and growing in his nearshore home.

About the Author

Kathleen Souza grew up in CT but now lives in Dartmouth, MA with her husband, Randy. Her first book, *August Skies*, was published in 2015. Inspired by her love of the ocean and its creatures and her admiration for those involved in sea turtle conservation, she has written *June Moon*.
Contact her at
junemoonbook@gmail.com
or visit *June Moon* on *Facebook*